TOWER HAMLETS

D0512488

BLOOMSBURY EDUCATION

Bloomsbury Publishing Plc

50 Bedford Square, London, WC1B 3DP, UK

BLOOMSBURY, BLOOMSBURY EDUCATION and the Diana logo are trademarks of
Bloomsbury Publishing Plc

First published in Great Britain 2018 by Bloomsbury Publishing Plc

Editor copyright © Joshua Seigal, 2018

Illustrations copyright © Tim Wesson, 2018

Joshua Seigal and Tim Wesson have asserted their rights under the Copyright, Designs
and Patents Act, 1988, to be identified as Author and Illustrator of this work

All rights reserved. No part of this publication may be reproduced or transmitted
in any form or by any means, electronic or mechanical, including photocopying,
recording, or any information storage or retrieval system, without prior permission
in writing from the publishers

A catalogue record for this book is available from the British Library

ISBN: PB: 978-1-4729-5548-7; ePDF: 978-1-4729-5547-0; ePub: 978-1-4729-5546-3

4   6   8   10   9   7   5   3

Text design by Janene Spencer

Printed and bound by CPI Group (UK) Ltd, Croydon CR0 4YY

MIX
Paper from
responsible sources
FSC® C020471

All papers used by Bloomsbury Publishing Plc are natural, recyclable products
from wood grown in well managed forests. The manufacturing processes conform
to the environmental regulations of the country of origin

**To find out more about our authors and books visit
www.bloomsbury.com and sign up for our newsletters**

I BET I CAN MAKE YOU LAUGH

POEMS BY JOSHUA SEIGAL AND FRIENDS

BLOOMSBURY EDUCATION

LONDON OXFORD NEW YORK NEW DELHI SYDNEY

Contents

I Bet I Can Make You Laugh

I bet I can make you laugh.
Are you ready?
Here goes:

.... *DEAD KITTENS!*

That didn't work, did it?
Okay, how about this.
Ready?

.... *ABANDONED PUPPIES!*

That didn't work either, did it?
Well, what about

.... *TERMINALLY ILL BUNNY RABBITS!*

No?
How about

.... *MASHED UP BUTTERFLIES!*

Or

.... *TEDDY BEARS IN THE RUBBISH DUMP!*

Or

.... *PARENTS THAT DON'T LOVE YOU!!!*

No?

You mean none of these things
is funny?

Hmmm.

Making you laugh
is harder than I thought.

Joshua Seigal

Introduction

I was delighted when Bloomsbury (the people who publish this book) asked me to put together an anthology of funny poems. After all, I have masses of hilarious poems, and the chance to get them all together in a big book was very exciting for me.

My joy evaporated, however, when Bloomsbury told me that it would be a small book, not a big book, and that I would have to invite lots of other poets to write poems for the book as well, as unfortunately they didn't think I was funny enough on my own.
After I'd finished crying, what I then had to do was ask a bunch of other poets to send me their poems so I could include a few in this book. About a thousand poets (and even one or two acrobats) sent me their poems, and I had to choose the best, funniest poems to be included. That is why the book you have in your hands is not by 'Joshua Seigal' but is

instead by 'Joshua Seigal and Friends'.
Now, I am friends with some of the other
poets in this book, but there are also some
poets I am not friends with. There are even
a few I have never met, and some very, very
old ones who are dead. When you get to be
an adult, one of the things you have to do is
pretend to be friends with lots of people, even
if you are not really friends with them at all.
That's just the way it is.

Anyway, I present to you a collection of
poems that I think are funny. Some of them
made me howl with laughter. Some of them
made me smile quietly to myself. Some of
them made me giggle. Some of them are very
clever. Some of them are very silly. Some of
them even made me think quite deeply.
And then you've got the poems by other
poets, some of which are quite good too...

J.S.

Words! Words! Words!

Hello. It's me again. I promise you can read some poems soon, but, before the hilarity begins, I'd like to say a little bit about how it's going to work.

I've divided the book into different sections. At the beginning of each section I am going to say some stuff, and then you can read the poems. I like saying stuff, and nobody can stop me.

This section is called 'Words! Words! Words!'. Words are amazing things. I think of words as toys, and to write a poem is to play with words. The poems in this section all do funny things with words. Hopefully they will **stretch** *your ideas about what words, and poems, can do.*

Enjoy!

J.S.

Knock, Knock

Knock, knock
Who's there?
A poet
A poet who?
A poet who dares share his poems with you...

Who once upon a time hid his rhyming inside
    him
Back when he was young he couldn't express
His sea-deep emotions. They only tongue-tied
    him
What he thought and he felt he left you to
    guess

Knock, knock
Who's there?
A poet
A poet who?
A poet who knows somewhere there's a poet
    in you

'Cos everyone here has a sense of rhythm
Everyone here wants a place to play
And sometimes we all need somebody to
    listen
To the words that we've got to say

Knock, knock
Who's there?
Europe
Europe who?
Hey, I'm not a poo!
I'm not even a pooet!
I'm a poet
And so are you.

Justin Coe

Goggles, Umbrella, Hullabaloo

Nobody knows who said the first word, or when
Or if they said it to themselves or a friend
Or a massive woolly mammoth they were
    chasing round a bend
Did words start out in songs?
Or with "ooh ooh! ah ah!" sounds like an ape?
Did someone yawn and it turned into a word by
    mistake?
From way back then to today
We've made up millions of words on the way
Not just "More!" or "Food!" or "No!"
Not just "Look out!" "Hello!" "Go!"
Not just "Scratch it!" "That bit!" "Slow!"
But words that make worlds on their own

For example, if you say that in a place called
    Art Town
the dogs only poop out purple paint
Or you write that
One time you ate a chicken nugget the size of
    a boulder
And it smelt of perfume

Or that you travelled here today on the back
    of a robot
Made from marshmallows
We can picture it,
Somewhere in our brain, it exists.
Which is brilliant isn't it? Words.
Also, some of them
just
  sound
     GOOD!

Goggles, umbrella, hullaballoo
Spaghetti, avalanche, doughnut,
Dusk, wallop, bash,
Dollop, blubber, zip.

Zip.
Zip. Zip.
Zip zip zip
Zip zip zip zip!

I love how it sounds!
I can't stop saying it.
Out of all the words in the world what's your
    favourite?

Say it aloud now, roll it round your mouth,
    feel the shape of it
Say it as slowly as you can
Really savour it, take in the taste of it
Now, is the flavour different if you say it
    quick?
Say it quick! Say it say it quick!
Zip zip zip zip zip zip zip

Simon Mole

The World's Worst Acrostic

Acrostic poems
Can be good.
Refrigerator.
Or they can be bad and
Spectacularly irrelevant.
iT seems that
I am not very good at them.
Can't you tell?

Carrie Esmond

First Drafts (Based on Famous Poems)

I wandered lonely as a
flatulent warthog.

Shall I compare thee to a
damp tea-towel?

If music be the food of love,
I have diarrhoea.

How do I love thee? Let me count
the muffins.

Water, water everywhere,
especially in the sink.

Tyger, Tyger,
you failed your spelling test.

What will survive of us is
potatoes.

Joshua Seigal

Rhyming

My teacher always said
a poem doesn't have to rhyme
but I like it when it does
so this one will, this time.

Dan Simpson

Discombobulated

I'm discombobulated
My head is in a mess
I went to school on Sunday
In nothing but my vest
I've eaten all my homework
It didn't taste too nice
I took a bath in gravy
And heated it with ice

I put my shoes on sideways
My trousers upside down
I called my teacher 'mummy'
Then lost a million pounds
I painted my hair purple
With stripes of shocking pink
I brushed my teeth with cabbage
Poured sardines in the sink

I whistled through my earholes
Slept on the garage floor
I heard a hamster barking
And saw a rabbit roar
I'm discombobulated
My brain is not plugged in
So now this poem is over
I'll throw it in the bin.

Neal Zetter

Not Exactly a Love Letter

You're the jam in my rice pudding.
(I prefer my pudding plain.)

You fill up all my thoughts.
(I've a headache in my brain.)

You're the tastiest steak there is.
(I've turned vegetarian.)

You're a happy song sung loudly.
(I'm an irritable librarian.)

You're the belt around my trousers.
(I'm sat nude in the bath.)

You're the world's best comedian.
(It only hurts when I laugh.)

You are my Pharaoh.
(I live in Ancient Greece.)

You've stolen my heart.
(I'm phoning the police.)

A. F. Harrold

You

You!
Your head is like a hollow drum.
You!
Your eyes are like balls of flame.
You!
Your ears are like fans for blowing fire.
You!
Your nostril is like a mouse's hole.
You!
Your mouth is like a lump of mud.
You!
Your hands are like drumsticks.
You!
Your belly is like a pot of bad water.
You!
Your legs are like wooden posts.
You!
Your backside is like a mountain-top.

Traditional, Igbo

So They Say

You can't make an omelette without breaking
    eggs,
You can't walk to school without using your
    legs,
You can't hang out washing without any pegs
(Unless you don't mind your undies hanging
    on next door's rose bushes).

Don't count your chickens before they hatch,
Don't play with fire – not even a match,
Don't throw cricket balls to friends
    who can't catch
(Especially if they're standing in front
    of a thin glass window).

Never look a gift horse in the mouth,
Never walk north if you want to go south,
Never start a verse if there isn't a routh
(Unless you can make up a new word that
    means 'rhyme')!

Celia Warren

On the Backwards Bus

gniog gnola
pots gnimoc pu
sserp nottub
sub gniwols
sub gnippots
gnidnats pu
gnippets tuo
emoh won

Hannah Whitley

The essential difference
between a screw and a nail
is that a screw is much harder
to hammer.

The essential difference
between broccoli and cauliflower
is that one is horrible
and the other is even worse.

The essential difference
between poems that make sense
and those that don't
is also broccoli.

Rob Walton

Would You Rather

Cuddle a walrus
or kiss a baboon?

Dive in the ocean
or fly to the moon?

Go out in winter
in only your pants,

or wash every night
in a bath full of ants?

Ride on a lion
or own a pet pig?

Shave all your hair off
or don a pink wig?

Never get homework
or always eat chips?

Sleep in an igloo
or live on a ship?

Twirl round and round
as you count up to ten,

or hear this poem
again and again

and again and again
and again and again?

Joshua Seigal

Dramatic Pause

I expect you want to know how this poem
ends
maybe I'll tell you in a while
or   after   stretching   out
every   last   word
perhaps

I'll end it here

or here

with a line break

there will be
an uncomfortable silence of course

foot and finger tapping are to be encouraged
those inclined to impatience
may shout

Come on get on with it!!!

Oh okay I will tell you soon

really
I promise

but then again I might just leave you

h
a
n
g
i
n
g

Sue Hardy-Dawson

School

School is important. You spend about 80 per cent of your life in school. That might not actually be true; I am not very good at percentages.
School is where you learn. For example, when I was at school I learnt how to pretend to need the toilet so I could waste some time during maths lessons. Had I spent more time in maths, I probably could have got a better job. And I might also be better at percentages.

Anyway. The poems in this section are about school. Sort of. What I mean to say is that they're a bit WEIRD.

J.S.

OOPS!

Yesterday, while getting dressed,
I made a foolish blunder.
It seems so simple, looking back,
I cannot help but wonder:
how on earth did I forget
that underpants go under?

Robert Schechter

Rules, Rules, Rules

No running
Rules, rules, rules, boring!

No talking
Rules, rules, rules, boring!

No pushing
Rules, rules, rules, boring!

No pinching
Rules, rules, rules, boring!

No nose picking
Rules, rules, rules, boring!

No TV watching
Rules, rules, rules, boring!

No computer game playing
Rules, rules, rules, boring!

No late night-ing
Rules, rules, rules, boring!

No yawning
Rules, rules, rules, boring!

No shouting
Rules, rules, rules, boring!

No ball kicking!
Rules, rules, rules, boring!

No open-mouth chewing
Rules, rules, rules boring!

No fidgeting!
Rules, rules, rules, boring!

No smiling, no laughing, no sniggering
no giggling, no chuckling,

Rules, rules, rules, boring!

Kat Francois

Yetification

When you wake up in your bed
and the feeling starts to spread
and you tingle deep inside –
you're becoming **YETIFIED!**

When your skin is growing hairy
and your feet are growing scary
and you're getting goggle-eyed –
you're becoming **YETIFIED!**

When your limbs are growing longer
and your face is getting wronger
and your chest is big and wide –
you're becoming **YETIFIED!**

When your throat begins to growl
and your mouth begins to howl
and your parents run and hide –
you're becoming **YETIFIED!**

When the people shout 'Beware!'
and the drivers gasp and stare
and their vehicles collide –
you're becoming **YETIFIED!**

When you look like you're all set
for the mountains of Tibet
only one thing is implied –
you're becoming **YETIFIED!**

When you're strutting round the school
and your classmates think you're cool
and you're puffed up full of pride –
you're becoming **YETIFIED!**

Now you're sizing up the teacher
and you get an urge to eat her.
No it cannot be denied...

You're becoming YETIFIED!

Joshua Seigal

Our Teacher is a Caveman

Our teacher is a caveman
With a long black scraggy beard
Although he is our fave man
He's wacky, wild and weird
Has limited vocabulary
Though great at ancient history
He doesn't go past 1 B.C.
Our teacher is a caveman

We call him Mr Ug
He's hairy and he's scary
And he waves a wooden club
He has a bath quite rarely
He's puzzled by the internet
He keeps a pterodactyl pet
That really does confuse the vet
Our teacher is a caveman

He lives deep in the forest
With his cave wife and cave child
He shows us how to sharpen spears
And how two sticks make fire

Some say his brain is very small
Won't use whiteboards, draws on walls
Come meet the school Neanderthal
Our teacher is a caveman

He loves to watch the Ice Age films
On TV every night
How did he ever get the job?
He cannot read or write
When teaching maths he counts with rocks
He owns a sundial but no clock
Check out his woolly mammoth socks
Our teacher is a caveman

Who cares if he's Palaeolithic?
We all think that he's terrific
Our teacher is a caveman.

Neal Zetter

My Homework Ate My Dog

My homework ate my dog, Miss!
My homework ate my dog!
I was doing it as ordered
And it croaked just like a frog,
The pages rippled open,
It had consonants for teeth,
I'm sure I saw a scale of vowels
Hidden underneath.

It rustled off the table
And it rustled past the door,
Its creepy undulations
Casting shadows on the floor.
I just sat right there and watched, Miss,
What else was I to do?
My homework ate my dog, Miss,
Before I even moved.

I promise I'm not lying, Miss,
That all of this is true,
I'd have brought my homework in
Except it tried to eat me too!

I'll start it all again, Miss,
And I'll have it in tomorrow,
As for my dog, don't worry,
There's another I can borrow.

Jay Hulme

To the Loo

I need to go
to the loo,
she said.
I need to go
to the loo!

*You're old enough
to know for sure
you really should
have gone before.*

It's just a wee.
I won't be long.
Oh, pretty pleeeease!
I can't hold on.

*You need to stop
this silly fuss.
Come on, Miss –
keep teaching us!*

James Carter

Ode to the Flu

I caught you going around
the staffroom like a tea round

you whispered into my body
and said you want to breed

bugs with me.
We last spoke in February,

when you stirred your mucus frappe
into slime on my chest.

You gave refuge
reminding me how to be warm

and stay in while you arrived
in my tissues with your yellow

after-party phlegm, swelling
my glands until I became

your wailing germ
bubbling in bacteria.

Tell doctors that I'm burning
in the style of a temperature.

This is how you saved me
from classroom torture

and jobs behind desks.
Tonight, in my sticky vest

drenched with a 3am
festival of sweat

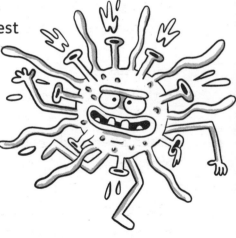

jiving
in a sick-bed

for you
I ache.

Raymond Antrobus

Home Life

When you are not at school you are probably at home with your family. They might be a regular family, with mums and dads and brothers and sisters and stuff like that. Or they might be an unusual family. Perhaps you live with a pack of warthogs. I won't judge you.

I used the word 'regular', but in fact there is not really such a thing as a regular home or family. All families are very, very strange. You might not think your family is strange, but I promise you that it is. You family is deeply odd, just like everyone else's.

The poems in this section are about family. The first poem, Daddy Fell into the Pond, is quite an old poem, and is in fact one of the poems I remember laughing at when I was little (about a million years ago).

Here goes...

Daddy Fell into the Pond

Everyone grumbled. The sky was grey.
We had nothing to do and nothing to say.
We were nearing the end of a dismal day,
And there seemed to be nothing beyond,
      THEN
  Daddy fell into the pond!

And everyone's face grew merry and bright,
And Timothy danced for sheer delight.
"Give me the camera, quick, oh quick!
He's crawling out of the duckweed."
      Click!

Then the gardener suddenly slapped his knee,
And doubled up, shaking silently,
And the ducks all quacked as if they were daft
And it sounded as if the old drake laughed.
O, there wasn't a thing that didn't respond
      WHEN
  Daddy fell into the pond!

Alfred Noyes

LOB

When Dad went out for a loaf of bread
He said BRB*
Eh? I said. Is that an acronym?
AFAIK** he replied.
TTYTT*** I'm not really sure
I just wanted to be DWTK****
DYTTC*****
I said
W******

*Be right back
** As far as I know
*** To tell you the truth
**** Down with the kids
***** Don't you think that's clever?
****** Whatever!

Roger Stevens

Sunday Morning Lion

On Sunday mornings
Mum and Dad
have a lion.
They say to us,
"we've been working hard
all week. Please don't
disturb us in the morning.
We need a lion."
When they get up
the lion is always gone.
I've never even seen
Mum and Dad's lion.
In fact
the next time
they have a lion
on a Sunday morning
this is what
I'm going to do:
I'm going to call to it.
I'm going to stand outside
Mum and Dad's room
and shout
RAAAAAAARRRRRGGGGGGHHHH!

Joshua Seigal

Lazybones

Lazybones, let's go to the farm
Sorry, I've got a headache
Lazybones, let's go pounding grain
Sorry, my leg isn't right
Lazybones, let's go fetch firewood
Sorry, my hands are hurting
Lazybones, come and have some food
Hold on, let me wash my hands!

Traditional, Malawi

You Are Old, Father William

"You are old, Father William," the young man
  said,
"And your hair has become very white;
And yet you incessantly stand on your head,
Do you think, at your age, it is right?"

"In my youth," Father William replied to his
  son,
"I feared it might injure the brain;
But, now that I'm perfectly sure I have none,
Why, I do it again and again."

"You are old," said the youth, "as I mentioned
  before,
And you have grown most uncommonly fat;
Yet you turned a back-somersault in at the
  door,
Pray what is the reason for that?"

"In my youth," said the sage, as he shook his
  grey locks,
"I kept all my limbs very supple

By the use of this ointment, one shilling a box,
Allow me to sell you a couple?"

"You are old," said the youth, "and your jaws
    are too weak
For anything tougher than suet;
Yet you finished the goose, with the bones
    and the beak,
Pray, how did you manage to do it?"

"In my youth," said his father, "I took to the
    law,
And argued each case with my wife;
And the muscular strength, which it gave to
    my jaw,
Has lasted the rest of my life."

"You are old," said the youth, "one would
    hardly suppose
That your eye was as steady as ever;
Yet you balanced an eel on the end of your
    nose,
What made you so awfully clever?"

"I have answered three questions, and that is
    enough,"
Said his father. "Don't give yourself airs!
Do you think I can listen all day to such stuff?
Be off, or I'll kick you down stairs."

Lewis Carroll

My Crazy Cousins

Cousin Jan, Cousin Jan,
drives around in an ice-cream van

Cousin Tim, Cousin Tim,
doesn't drive, prefers to swim

Cousin Mike, Cousin Mike,
rides along on a purple bike

Cousin Hans, Cousin Hans,
struts around in orange pants

Cousin Hugo, Cousin Hugo,
goes where I go, goes where you go

Cousin Russell, Cousin Russell,
a car won't suit him, but a bus'll

Cousin Felicity, Cousin Felicity,
motorised by electricity

Cousin Martin, Cousin Martin,
eats baked beans, does lots of...

Joshua Seigal

Note to My Napping Sister

Dear Sis, we share a family name.
Our looks are close but not the same.

At school the teachers think I'm you!
Doesn't that annoy you, too?

Never again, I'm proud to report.
(Sorry I cut your hair so short)

Karen G. Jordan

What I Want for Christmas

Last year I got a bicycle.
I rode it for a while.
The year before I got a phone
that soon went out of style.
My friends are getting football shirts
but I'm less orthodox:
what I want for Christmas
is a lovely pair of socks...

Fancy socks, swanky socks,
dirty, stinky, skanky socks,
teenage brother's manky socks,
Socks! Socks! Socks!

Stripy socks, silly socks,
dainty socks and frilly socks,
socks for when I'm chilly socks,
Socks! Socks! Socks!

I used to have a Batman suit
but I grew out of it,
I used to have a spaceman costume

but the gusset split.
What I've set my heart on now,
it won't be hard to finance;
what I want for Christmas
is a pair of mighty fine pants.

Tight pants, stretchy pants,
beautiful and fetching pants,
big pants, pink pants,
Pants! Pants! Pants!

Loose pants, saggy pants,
big and beige and baggy pants,
pants just like my granny has,
Pants! Pants! Pants!

My mum has asked for flowers
and my dad has asked for books,
but when I say what I want
then I get some funny looks.
You may think I'm peculiar,
you may think I'm offbeat,
but what I want for Christmas
is a brand-new toilet seat.

Shiny ones, bold ones,
silver ones and gold ones,
ruby ones, diamond ones,
Toi! Let! Seats!

Flash ones, cool ones,
sparkly ones and jewelled ones,
like they have at school ones
Toi! Let! Seats!

You may well think I'm dumb
but it's where I put my bum,
so let me have some fun
with a brand
new
toi
let
seeeeeaaaaat!

Yeah!

Joshua Seigal

Go and Get a Haircut

Go and get a haircut,
It's looking rather long,
Go and ask the barber
He'll tell you I'm not wrong.
It's just that I prefer it
Not covering your face,
Go and get a haircut
And I'll be off your case.

Go and get a haircut.
Go and make it neat.
It's grown beyond your shoulders
It's grown beyond your feet.
You can measure it in metres
You can measure it in miles
Go and get a haircut,
Try out other styles.

Go and get a haircut!
It's getting out of hand!
It's spread across the county
It's spread across the land.

You're mentioned on the internet
You're mentioned on the news.
Go and get it cut,
I've got a chainsaw you can use!

Go and get a haircut,
The army's mobilized!
Reports suggest there's many dead,
By that I'm not surprised!
The Prime Minister's requested,
That you have a little trim;
That you go and get a haircut
And I agree with him!

Go and get a haircut,
Evacuations have begun.
We're abandoning the planet
We're off to find another one.
I'm off to catch a spaceship
But in case you do decide
To go and get a haircut,
I've left a tenner on the side.

Andrew McWhirter

How Not to Impersonate Your Mum on the Telephone

Swimming
The worst day of the week
Mum refused to write a note
So...

I practised in the mirror
The facial expression
That high-pitched screeching whine
"My Benjamin is so ill today!"
"My Benjamin has such a fever!"

I looked like Mum
I sounded like Mum
I was Mum!

So...
Picked up the telephone...
Dialled the number...
Deep breath and...
"Hello!
This is my mum speaking!"
Oops!

Debra Bertulis

Cartoons

One day I'll grow up
and I'll have to live life.
I might finish school
and I might find a wife.
It might happen later,
it might happen soon
but one thing's for sure:
I'll keep watching cartoons.

I might ditch my trainers
and wear a smart suit.
I might get a job
where I have to commute.
I might be a spaceman
and fly to the moon
but don't be in doubt:
I'll keep watching cartoons.

I might be a doctor,
curing disease.
I might be a lumberjack,
hacking down trees.

I might be a zookeeper
taming baboons
but never you fear:
I'll keep watching cartoons.

My hair might turn grey
and my joints might go creaky.
My mind might go blank
and my bladder go leaky.
I might lose my teeth
and eat mush with a spoon
but as I expire
I'll be watching cartoons.

With the WOWS!
and the POWS!
and the ZAPS!
and the ZOOMS!
no I'll never stop watching cartoons!

Joshua Seigal

The Howling

Our baby is howling,
it just isn't right,
he howls and he howls
all day and all night.

He howls when he's wet,
he howls when he's dry,
he howls and he howls
and he doesn't know why.

He howls at our mum
he howls at our dad,
the howling, the howling,
it's driving us mad.

Then one night, he changes!
As we stand and stare,
our baby stops howling
and starts growing hair.

Hair grows on his fingers,
hair grows on his toes,
hair grows on his ears
and all over his nose.

Look at his teeth!
Look at his nails!
Our baby's so happy
he's wagging his tail.

Outside, shadows shift
in the silvery gloom.
As the clouds roll away,
he howls at the moon.

Our baby's got it!
He's got it right.
We only howl when
the moon's full and bright.

Our baby's a werewolf,
just like me and you.
Let's join in the howling.
Arooo-ooo-ooo-ooo!

Jane Clarke

Animals

Animals are great, aren't they? Deep down, we are all animals. Some of us more than others.

I started writing a lot about animals when we got our first dog, a Lhasa apso named Winston (or Wini-Woodles for short). Lhasa apsos come from Tibet, and the words 'Lhasa apso' mean something like 'hairy Tibetan barking dog that looks cute but will probably bite you'.

In this section you will find lots of poems about animals. There are some dog poems, but also ones about more exotic, exciting animals like pigeons, vultures and teachers.
(Actually, come to think of it, I put the teacher poems in the 'School' section. Maybe I should have put them here instead.)

J.S.

Dog Translations

Grrrrwffwffwfff – I'm hungry
Hrrr hrrrr hrrrr – Please rub my belly
ARRRHARRRAOOOWWW! – Wow! A full moon!
Wuff! Wuff! – Walkies! Walkies!
Hmmmm! Hmmmmmmmm? – Can I have
    your sandwich?
Hmmmhhmmmmmmm?! – Please?!
Huhuhuhuhuh! – I'm tired
App! App! App! – Stop playing on your phone
    and pay me attention
Miaow! – Look! I'm a cat!

Joshua Seigal

Dogmatic!

I've got a new DogMatic –
she's my automatic pet.
Of all the beasts I've ever bought
she is the best one yet.
She likes to play outside with me
but sometimes she gets wet,
and then she blows her circuitry
and ends up at the vet.

I've got a new DogMatic –
she's my high-performance mate.
Of all the cronies I could own
it's her I really rate.
I simply click a button
and she starts to calculate
the distance to the park, in metres,
from our garden gate.

I've got a new DogMatic –
she's my electronic chum.
She's smarter than my sister,
more efficient than my mum.
She has a byte at dinner time
and then, when she is done,
a tiny little microchip
comes plopping out her bum...

Joshua Seigal

Monkey See, Monkey Do

Monkey see, monkey do,
Monkey free from monkey zoo.

Monkey up, monkey down,
Monkey run to monkey town.

Monkey smell monkey eats,
Monkey find monkey treats.

Monkey taste monkey buns,
Monkey scoff monkey tons.

Monkey full, monkey stuffed,
Monkey slow, monkey puffed.

Monkey need monkey loo,
Monkey wee, monkey poo.

Monkey slip, monkey call,
Monkey down, monkey fall.

Monkey see, monkey do,
Monkey back in monkey zoo.

Andy Seed

Crab

Crab with a small brain
Why do you
Go backward
To go forward?
Is it my own world
Is it your own world
Which is upside down?
Lucky you are not a car
Otherwise,
Oh dear, oh dear,
You would have so many accidents!

Irene Assiba D'Almeida

If you want to annoy my dog
(and I mean really, really annoy him),
don't bother taking his dinner.
He'll look bemused, maybe let out
a whine, but he can handle it.

Nor is it any use to snatch his toy,
or to cut short his walk –
these things are minor grievances
which he will face with patience.

No, if you want to really, really annoy my dog
just blow
        very softly
                on his head.

He'll bristle and yelp
and bat the breeze with his paws...

He'll snuffle and yap
and snap at the gust with his jaws...

If you want to really, really annoy my dog,
a tiny little puff of air
will get him as growly
as a grizzly bear.

And it isn't just my dog:
if you want to really, really annoy my dad
just do what I do

and climb in bed with him,
on a Sunday morning,
and blow
        very gently
                in his face...

Joshua Seigal

Shrew

Shrew so
shrewy shrewd
shrewyshrewrysh...

shhhh!

shy shrew shurrush
shurrush

shhh scatter-rush
nibbly heartrace
shy shrew, rue
crooow, crue, corrow, crooow-crow-go!

rush hush shussshhh
wry wrynecked shrewy shrew
    nested,
        rested,
            stewed shrew

Sarah Westcott

Panda Versus Penguin

Panda versus penguin,
it's the battle of the black and white.
The panda is a bear
that's about to become extinct
and the penguin is a bird
who has lost the power of flight.

Panda versus penguin,
it's the fight of the century.
The penguin has no hands
so he cannot throw a punch
and the panda will be sleeping,
if he's not eating his lunch.

Panda versus penguin,
you'd better get your tickets now,
because the ice-caps are shrinking
the panda is extincting* –
leave it too long and you'll
    be watching
seagull versus cow.

Angela Cleland

*Not actually a word, kids. Also, a biologist friend tells me that the panda
may be out of the woods – not literally out of the woods, but figuratively out
of the woods – and that penguins actually do OK in sunnier climates, so this
poem is obsolete and mildly inaccurate. Still, it just goes to show that if you
do make a mistake, like driving a species to the brink of extinction, it's always
worth having a go at clearing up your mess.

Nature Trail

Went on a nature trail
Went wiv me class
Had to look fer animals
an bits of grass

Brung back an hedgehog
pizzaflat an dead.
"Whatever has come over you?"
the teacher said.

(It was probally a lorry
by the look of his head.)

Sarah Smith

Wattle I Do?

When I awoke this morning
there were feathers in my bed.
A beady little pair of eyes
was bulging in my head.

I tried to shout for help
but I just clucked; I couldn't speak.
My mouth had been supplanted
by a little pointy beak.

My arms had turned to wings.
My comb was difficult to hide.
My mum made eggs for breakfast –
when she scrambled them I cried.

This morning I felt fowl
from my head down to my socks.
I hope that I recover
from this bout of chicken pox.

Joshua Seigal

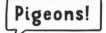

Pigeons! on the pavement
Pigeons! in the sky
Pigeons! in the garden
Pigeons! going by
Pigeons! flapping wings and
Pigeons! pecking bread
Pigeons! in conspiracy
Pigeons! overhead

*Wherever you go
and whatever you do,
better watch out
it's **PIGEON POO!***

Pigeons! on the street and
Pigeons! in the square
Pigeons! over here and
Pigeons! over there
Pigeons! in the muck and
Pigeons! in the bin
Pigeons! with a smirk and
Pigeons! with a grin

Wherever you go
and whatever you do,
better watch out
*it's **PIGEON POO!***

Pigeons! in the rain and
Pigeons! in the sun
Pigeons! being nasty
Pigeons! having fun
Pigeons! in the puddles
Pigeons! in the trees
Pigeons! with the lurgy
Pigeons! with disease

Wherever you go
and whatever you do,
better watch out
it's...

Joshua Seigal

Food

Not many things in life are certain, but one of them is this: if you do not eat food you will die. Another thing that is certain is that if you eat my mum's cooking, you will also die.

If you read the poems in this section you might die, but it will be of laughter. For not only is food tasty (unless it is my mum's food), it can also be very funny. So sit back, make yourself a nice, hot, steaming mug of cow's mucus mixed with mashed-up jungle beans* and enjoy.

*otherwise known as hot chocolate

J.S.

Say Cheese!

Say Stilton
Say Cheddar
Say Jarlsberg
Say Feta
Say fresh Mozzarella
Say CHEESE!

Say Yarg
Say Halloumi
Say Greve
Say Sulguni
Say So
Say Nguri
Say CHEESE!

Say Dragon's Breath Blue
Say Petits Filous
Say smelly Vieux
Say CHEESE!

Help spread the word
Of milk, whey and curd
Haven't you heard?
I said CHEESE!

Joshua Seigal

The Value of an Onion

Always keep an onion handy.
They're great for self-defence.

If someone tries to beat you up,
whip out your onion and say,

"Look! Behold! An onion!
The Great Onion of Dreams!

The Magic Onion of Derek*!
Stare upon it and shudder!

For it is an astonishing onion!
An Onion of Power and Fear!

Gaze upon its majesty in awe!
Tremble before this Onion!"

And then, when the bully's thoroughly confused
kick them in the shin and run away.

*Insert your own name, or another name of your
choice that you think sounds impressive.*

A. F. Harrold

Oh Sausage

Oh sausage, you are my best friend,
you've got a perfect round little bottom!
One at each end.
Oh sausage, I wish that you could talk
I wish you could tell me your dreams, hopes,
fears and thoughts,
but all you ever seem to want to do is...
get chased round plates by knives and forks.
Oh sausage, when you get tired
I will put you gently to bed,
tell you a night-time story, sing you a sweet
dreams lullaby,
then wrap you up all snuggily between two
slices of bread
and when you are fast asleep –
I'll bite off your head.

Paul Lyalls

Menu for Monsters

Starters:
>   Creepy-crawly canapés
>   Swamp soup with extra slime
>   Mushrooms stuffed with maggots
>   Toenails tossed in grime

Main Courses:
>   Frogs' eye-balls in gravy
>   Raw fish with flabby lips
>   Belly of boiled dinosaur
>   Fried slug with greasy chips

Desserts:
>   Skunk pie with lumpy custard
>   Frosted fleas and lice
>   Spiders' legs in jelly
>   Sugared rats and mice

Annie Fisher

On the Menu

Theo says his dad eats humans.
He ate the Johnsons and the Newmans.

He wolfed the Wolffs and fried the Foxes;
he slurped the Smiths and nibbled the
        Knoxes.

He cooked the Cooksons' brains in oil
and roasted the Richards' in silver foil.

He attacked the Ahmeds with ravenous glee
and gobbled the Greens with grapes and brie.

He boiled the Baileys and potted the Potters;
he chopped up the Changs in a bowl of pigs'
        trotters.

He goes hunting for Hunters like he's hunting
        for grouse
and we've been invited to Theo's house.

Joshua Seigal

The Perils of Breakfast

Watch out for bears in your cornflakes.

Bears are dangerous.
Bears have big claws.
Bears are always hungry.
At breakfast time, doubly so.

If you lift a spoonful of cornflakes to your mouth
and it's got a bear hiding in it,
well,
you'll be in trouble, then. Won't you?
Eaten up just like that.
Gobble. Gobble. Crunch.

Fortunately
bears are larger than cornflakes
and so you can usually spot
a little bit of fur poking round the side.

If you do
spot a little bit of fur poking round the side
just put your spoon down,
step away
and have something else for breakfast
instead.

But,
watch out for crocodiles in your porridge
and watch out for tigers under your toast.

A. F. Harrold

Season's Eatings

An angry voice erupted
from my oven with a shout:
"It's much too warm inside this place!
You have to let me out!"

It sounded quite irate
but then, when all is said and done,
it can't be very nice to be
a hot, cross bun.

Joshua Seigal

Phat Bucks

A man with skinny legs
walked into a skinny shop
ordered a skinny cappuccino
and a skinny chocolate chip muffin to go.
The skinny waitress said "that will be a fiver."
He pulled his skinny wallet from his pocket
paid the waitress with a skinny smile
She took the money and placed it in the phat till.

Adisa

Leftovers

Don't worry, we're nearly finished. There's just one more section to go, and then you can get on with something more useful, like feeding your pet wombat or juggling mangoes.

This final section is basically full of poems that didn't fit in anywhere else. I gathered them all up together, gave them a cuddle, and stuck them at the end. A bit like my parents used to do to me.

Some of the poems in this section are a bit random. Others are the kinds of poems that I thought seemed to work at the end of a book. I don't know why – they just have that 'endy' feel about them.

J.S

Where Are You Going?

I'm going to see a man about a dog
I'm off to race a snail and a slug
I'm going to pin a tail on the donkey
And when I get back?
I'll give you a hug

I'm going to catch a lobster by the tail
I'm off to find the middle of next week
I'm going to cut the lawn with nail scissors
And when I get back?
A kiss on the cheek.

I'm going to skateboard down the Eiffel Tower
I'm off to ask a wise man for some tips
I'm going to climb the mountains on the moon
And when I get back?
A kiss on the lips.

I'm going to Paradise (just north of Croydon)
I'm off to pick a California poppy
I'm going to swim with dolphins, and with
    haddock
And when I get back?
A kiss, wet and sloppy.

Roger Stevens

Prince Not-So-Charming

Prince Charming's turned into a creep.
He's made a few princesses weep.
He gives them a kiss,
but leans down to hiss,
"You could do with some more beauty sleep!"

Rebecca Colby

Things Could Be Worse

There could be ninja cats
hiding in the wardrobe

There could be three horses
chewing at the curtains

A flock of crows might
carry off the ceiling

The bed might be alive
and very hungry

Our fingers might belong
to someone in Australia
who practises
the piano all day long

Our eyes might only see
inside the stomach of
an ostrich in Sudan

Our thoughts might be perpetually confused
with those of an angry marmoset
so everything we think
is full of fruit and branches
and our missing tail

Cheer up.

Huw Evans

Seaside Collective

On the beach
within reach
of the soft, wet slap
of grey lace lap
round the mouth of
an incoming tide,

a carelessness of shoes,
a sanding of socks,
a soaking of shorts
and a hiding of hoodies,

lie astride
a rust grizzled pipe

near a pattern of pants,
all with circular patches
where a cheek
of wet buttocks
once sat.

Janet Philo

Moongazing

I stare at the moon
The moon stares back

Every night we play stares
Me and the moon

It ripples its surface
I stick out my tongue

It waxes and wanes
I blow raspberries

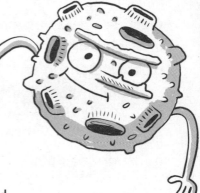

Some time later
We get tired and agree

Rest for staring eyes
and starry skies required

Bedtime for both
A truce, a tie

The battle goes on
Tomorrow, tomorrow.

Gary W. Hartley

Impatience

When I kiss a girl.
Still waiting.

When I grow a beard.
Still waiting.

When I get a job.
Still waiting.

When I have a child.
Still waiting.

When I'm in my grave.
Still waiting.

When my skull is cracked.
Still waiting.

When I turn to dust.
Still waiting.

STILL WAITING!

Frank Dixon (aged 7)

Bottom

Saggy, squidgy, baggy bum,
Bopping, bouncy, boogie bum.

Wiggly, jiggly, cheeky bum,
Sporty, perky, peachy bum.

Flashy, funky, trendy bum,
Simply, dimply, pimply bum.

Achy, shaky, wobbly bum,
Rumpus, trump us, windy bum.

A rump, a rear, backend,
Buttocks, bottom,

The end.

Lorraine Dancer

Acknowledgements

The following poems have been reproduced by kind permission of the poets.

'Phat Bucks' © Adisa. 'Ode to the Flu' Raymond Antrobus. 'Crab' © Irene Assiba D'Almeida. 'How Not to Impersonate Your Mum on the Telephone © Debra Bertulis. 'To The Loo' © James Carter 2018. 'The Howling' © Jane Clarke. 'Panda Versus Penguin' © Angela Cleland. 'Knock, Knock' © Justin Coe. 'Prince Not-So-Charming' © Rebecca Colby. 'Bottom' © Lorraine Dancer. 'Impatience' © Frank Dixon. 'The World's Worst Acrostic' © Carrie Esmond. 'Things Could Be Worse' © Huw Evans. 'Menu for Monsters' © Annie Fisher. 'Rules, Rules, Rules' © Kat Francois. 'Dramatic Pause' © Sue Hardy-Dawson. 'Not Exactly a Love Letter' and 'The Perils of Breakfast' © A. F. Harrold. First published in *Things You Find In A Poet's Beard* (Burning Eye Books, 2015), reproduced by kind permission of the poet. 'The Value of An Onion' © A. F. Harrold. 'Moongazing' © Gary W. Hartley. 'My Homework Ate My Dog' © Jay Hulme. 'Note to My Napping Sister' © Karen G. Jordan. 'Oh Sausage' © Paul Lyalls. 'Go and Get A Haircut' © Andrew McWhirter. 'Goggles, Umbrella, Hullabaloo' © Simon Mole. 'Daddy Fell into the Pond' © Alfred Noyes, by kind permission of The Society of Authors as the Literary Representative of the Estate of Alfred Noyes. 'Seaside Collective' © Janet Philo. 'OOPS!' © Robert Schechter. 'Monkey See Monkey Do' © Andy Seed, 2017, by permission of the author. 'Cartoons', 'Dogmatic!', 'Dog Translations', 'First Drafts (Based on Famous Poems)', 'I Bet I Can Make You Laugh', 'My Crazy Cousins', 'On The

Menu', 'Pigeons!', 'Say Cheese!', 'Season's Eatings', 'Sunday Morning Lion', 'Vexing Rex', 'Wattle I Do?', 'What I Want for Christmas,' 'Would You Rather' and 'Yetification' © Joshua Seigal. 'Rhyming' © Dan Simpson. 'Nature Trail' © Sarah Smith. 'LOB' and 'Where Are You Going?' © Roger Stevens. 'The Essentials' © Rob Walton. 'So They Say' © Celia Warren 2018. 'Shrew' © Sarah Westcott. 'On the Backwards Bus © Hannah Whitley. 'Discombobulated' and 'Our Teacher is a Caveman' © Neal Zetter.

All possible care has been taken to trace the ownership of each poem included in this selection and to obtain copyright permissions for its use, but in some cases copyright proved untraceable. If any omissions or errors have occurred, the publisher offers their apologies and will make the necessary corrections in subsequent editions.

I DON'T LIKE POETRY

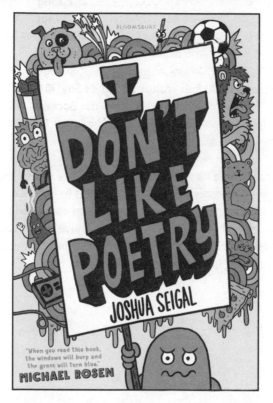

With poems on every topic from the power of books to the joys of fried chicken, the brilliant debut collection from Joshua Seigal was shortlisted for the 2017 Laugh Out Loud Awards – the UK's only prize for funny children's books. If you like poetry, you'll like this book. And if you don't like poetry you'll LOVE it!

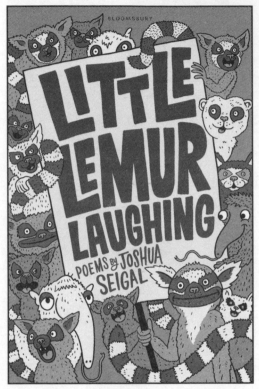

Funny, engaging and a little bit silly, this fantastic collection of poems has something to get everyone excited about poetry. Watch out – pretty soon you'll be laughing like a lemur!